ALEXANDER MCCALL SMITH

The *Mystery* of the
Missing Lion

Alexander McCall Smith is the author of
the No. 1 Ladies' Detective Agency series,
the Isabel Dalhousie series, the Portuguese
Irregular Verbs series, the 44 Scotland
Street series, and the Corduroy Mansions
series. He was born in what is now known
as Zimbabwe and lives in Scotland, where
in his spare time he is a bassoonist in the
RTO (Really Terrible Orchestra).

www.alexandermccallsmith.com

BOOKS IN THE NO. 1 LADIES' DETECTIVE AGENCY SERIES

The No. 1 Ladies' Detective Agency

Tears of the Giraffe

Morality for Beautiful Girls

The Kalahari Typing School for Men

The Full Cupboard of Life

In the Company of Cheerful Ladies

Blue Shoes and Happiness

The Good Husband of Zebra Drive

The Miracle at Speedy Motors

Tea Time for the Traditionally Built

The Double Comfort Safari Club

The Saturday Big Tent Wedding Party

The Limpopo Academy of Private Detection

The Minor Adjustment Beauty Salon

The Handsome Man's De Luxe Café

FOR CHILDREN

The Great Cake Mystery

The Mystery of Meerkat Hill

Alexander McCall Smith

The Mystery of the Missing Lion

Alexander McCall Smith

The Mystery of the Missing Lion

A Precious Ramotswe
Mystery for Young Readers

Illustrated by Iain McIntosh

Anchor Books   A Division of Random House LLC   New York

AN ANCHOR BOOKS ORIGINAL, OCTOBER 2014

Copyright © 2013 by Alexander McCall Smith
Illustrations copyright © 2013 by Iain McIntosh

All rights reserved. Published in the United States by
Anchor Books, a division of Random House LLC, and in Canada by
Random House of Canada Limited, Toronto, Penguin Random House
companies. Originally published in Great Britain as
Precious and the Mystery of the Missing Lion by Polygon, an imprint
of Birlinn Ltd., Edinburgh, in 2013.

The Cataloging-in-Publication Data is available at the
Library of Congress.

Anchor Books Trade Paperback ISBN: 978-0-8041-7327-8
eBook ISBN: 978-0-8041-7328-5
Hardcover ISBN: 978-1-1018-7202-4
Gibraltar Library ISBN: 978-1-1018-7203-1

www.anchorbooks.com

Printed in the United States of America
10 9 8 7 6 5 4 3 2 1

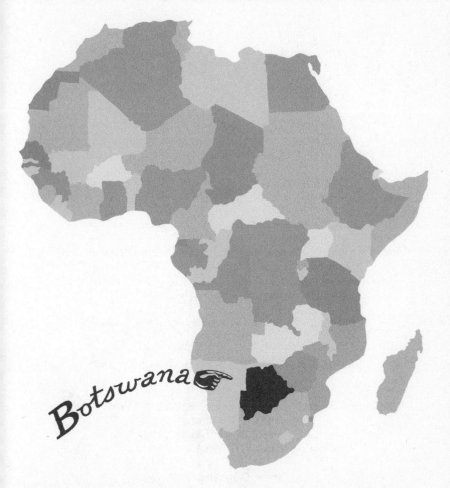

Botswana

THE GIRL IN THIS PICTURE is called Precious. That was her first name, and her second name was Ramotswe, and when all this happened she was nine. Nine is a good age to be. Some people like being nine so much that they really want to stay that age forever. They usually turn ten, however, and then they find out that being ten is not all that bad either. Precious, of course, was very happy being nine.

Like many of us, Precious had a number of aunts—three in fact. One of these aunts lived in the village in Botswana where

Precious was born, while another lived on an ostrich farm almost one hundred miles away. And a third, who was probably her favorite aunt of all, lived right up at the top of the country, in a place called the Okavango Delta. That's a lovely name, isn't it? Try saying it. OKA-VANGO.

A delta, of course, is made up of small rivers spreading out from a bigger river, a little bit like a human hand and its fingers.

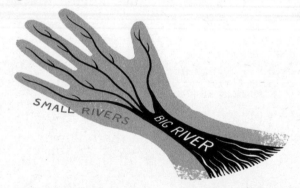

Usually deltas are on the edge of the sea—this one was not. The great Okavango River flowed *backward*—away from the sea, to spread out into smaller streams that simply sank into the sands of

a desert. And where this happened, there were wide plains of golden grass dotted with trees. On the bank of the river itself, the trees towered high. That was a bit like a proper jungle, and you had to be very careful when making your way through it. It was all very wild, and was home to just about every sort of wild animal to be found in Africa.

The aunt who lived up there was called Aunty Bee. Precious had been told her real name, but had forgotten it. Nobody ever called Aunty Bee anything but Bee. It was just the way it was.

Aunty Bee was not one of those aunts who scold you or tell you what to do. She was fun. She was also very generous and never forgot to send Precious a present on her birthday. And what presents these were! They were all made by Aunty Bee herself, from things that she could pick up in the bush around her.

One year there was a hat made entirely out of porcupine quills. As you know, porcupines are very prickly animals that have coats made of extraordinary black-and-white quills. These are sharp, and if anything tries to attack the porcupine all that he has to do is shoot out these quills. The animal attacking him then learns a very painful lesson: do not try to eat a porcupine! Indeed, some say that this is the very first lesson that a mother lion or leopard teaches her children: *do not try to eat a porcupine!* Unfortunately, some of them do not listen:

The porcupine hat was made of quills that Aunty Bee had found lying around on a path. She picked these up and took them to make into a hat.

Precious was very proud of it.

"What a beautiful hat," people remarked. "May we touch it?"

"Yes," said Precious. "But I wouldn't, if I were you!"

Another present Aunty Bee sent one year was a bracelet made of twisted elephant hair. This was very special, as people said that elephant hair was lucky.

Such bracelets were also very rare, as the elephant hair had to be plucked from the end of the elephant's tail, and it was very dangerous to do that. Elephants do not like you to pull their tails, even if all you want is to borrow a few hairs for a bracelet.

Aunty Bee bought that elephant hair from a man who was very thin. People said that an elephant had sat on him and squashed him a bit, but nobody knew whether or not that was true. But it certainly made an interesting story to tell to people who admired the bracelet.

And there were other presents, too. There was a cup made out of the seedpod of a great baobab tree. These trees are very wide and fat: so wide that it can take twenty people holding hands to go all the way round them. Think of that! Twenty people!

It was not just on her birthday that Precious heard from her Aunty Bee. Often a letter would arrive with news of what was happening up at the safari camp

where she worked. A safari camp is a place where people go to make trips into the wilderness. They go out for days on end to see wild animals and take photographs of them. They live in tents and eat out in the open and usually enjoy themselves very much indeed.

The camp that Aunty Bee worked in was called Eagle Island Camp. She was one of the cooks there, but she also earned a bit of money telling stories to the visitors. She knew all the old Botswana stories and would recite these beside the fireside at night. People loved to hear these and would clap and clap after she finished.

Aunty Bee was very busy but she always seemed to find the time to write to Precious, even if the letters were not very long—one or two lines perhaps. And it was in one of these short letters that she asked Precious whether she would like to come up to visit her.

"Dear Precious," she wrote, "I know that the school holidays are coming up soon. Would you like to come and stay with me up at the safari camp for a few days? Something very exciting is about to happen. I do hope you can come. With love, Aunty Bee."

How would you answer a letter like that? Exactly—so would I!

HEN PRECIOUS showed this letter to her father, Obed Ramotswe, he looked doubtful.

"It's a long way away," he said. "It takes a whole day to get there—sometimes more."

"I don't mind," said Precious. "There are buses that go that way, aren't there?"

Obed scratched his head. "That costs money," he said. "And I've had a lot of bills to pay this month."

Precious tried not to show her disappointment. Her father was kind to her, and she knew that he would do anything to make her happy. If he said that there was no money for the bus fare, then she knew that this would be true.

"Perhaps I can go some other time," she said quietly. "I'll write to Aunty Bee and tell her."

Obed held up a hand. "No," he said. "Don't do that. I think I may know somebody who's going up there for four or five days. He's a cattle buyer and he has some business to do in those parts. He might be able to give you a ride up in his truck."

Precious hardly dared hope. "Do you think so?" she asked. "I wouldn't take up much room."

Her father smiled. "I'll ask him," he said. "He owes me a favor, anyway."

That evening, Precious wrote a reply to her aunt telling her that there was a chance—just a chance—she would be able to come to stay with her. The next day, though, even before she had time to post this letter, her father went to have a word with his friend. When he returned to the house, he was full of smiles.

"You can do your packing," he said. "You're going to be leaving tomorrow."

Precious was too excited to go to sleep easily that night. Eventually she dropped off, and dreamed that she was already up in the Delta. There were tall trees, and these trees were full of monkeys, swinging adventurously from every branch. There was a wide river, filled with clear, swift-flowing water, and in this water there were the long dark shapes of crocodiles and fat, floating hippos. There were wide plains of

high grass, and in this grass, half-hidden
and staring out with large yellow eyes,
there were lions.

She awoke to her father's voice.

"Time to get up, my darling," he said.
"The truck will be here any moment
now."

She leapt out of bed and dressed quickly.
Her father had made her a breakfast of
thick porridge and goat's milk, and she
ate this while he checked that she had
everything she needed. There was a little
bit of money—not much—tied up in an old

handkerchief. "You can use that to buy yourself a treat," he said.

She wiped the traces of milk from her lips. "I'll buy you a present," she said.

"You don't need to do that," he said, smiling. "You may need some food on the way. Use it for something like that."

There came the sound of a horn from the road outside.

"That'll be the truck," said her father. "Off you go, now."

Obed's friend was called Mr. Poletsi. He was traveling with his wife, who was called Mma Poletsi, and there were ten passengers—friends and friends of

friends—who had crowded into the back of the truck. The Poletsis sat in the front, in the cab, while everybody else made themselves as comfortable as they could in the back. There were also several chickens in a small coop, a dog tied to somebody's toe with a piece of string, and a baby goat. Precious thought it a very strange mixture, but the important thing for her was that she was on her way to see her aunt. That was all that mattered, she thought.

In spite of the fact that the truck was crowded, everybody seemed to be in a

good mood and very happy to be traveling together. Some of the others had brought food with them, and this they shared with their fellow passengers. Precious knew that this was very important. She had been taught to share, as people are taught in Africa, and if she had had any food with her she would have shared it too.

At the beginning of the journey, it was cool enough sitting in the back of the truck, but as the day wore on it became hotter and hotter. Now, with the midday sun directly above them in the sky, it became very uncomfortable for the passengers and Precious would have given anything to be sitting in the comfort of the cab with the Poletsis, but she knew that this was impossible.

They stopped at a small store along the side of the road and they were able to have a long drink of water before continuing. This helped, but after half an hour or so she began to feel thirsty again.

"I hope we arrive soon," she said to the woman sitting beside her.

The woman laughed. "Oh, we won't arrive soon," she said. "We've still got hundreds of miles to go."

"When will we arrive?" asked Precious.

"Midnight, I think," said the woman. "Not before."

The road was straight and narrow, with very little traffic on it. For mile after mile it ran across great empty plains that stretched out on either side as far as

the eye could see. And it was while they were crossing one of these plains that the truck's engine suddenly coughed and died. One moment it was working and the next moment there was silence as the truck drew slowly to a halt.

They all got out. Mr. Poletsi opened the front of the truck and looked at the engine. He soon enough found the problem—a broken fanbelt. "This is very bad," he said. "We'll have to wait until somebody comes past. Then I can ask them to take me to the nearest town. I'll find a new fanbelt and come back with it."

"But that could take hours," said one of the passengers. "We may be here the whole night."

"I see no other way," said Mr. Poletsi. And then he added: "Unless anybody else has got any bright ideas?"

Precious looked at the fanbelt. It had been a complete circle, a bit like a massive elastic band—now it was just a single strip of rather sad-looking rubber.

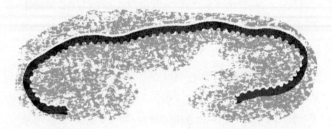

She looked down. She was wearing the belt that her father had bought her a few weeks before. She was very proud of it, but this was clearly an emergency.

"Has anybody got some string?" she asked.

The woman who had been sitting beside her replied that she had some and passed it to her.

Precious took off her belt. Carefully threading the string through one of the holes in the belt, she made it into a strong circle, exactly the size of the broken fanbelt.

Mr. Poletsi was watching her. "You clever girl," he exclaimed. "I can see what you're doing."

The makeshift fanbelt fit perfectly. Mr. Poletsi then closed the engine compartment and went back to his place in the cab. There was an anxious moment as everybody waited to see whether the truck would start. But it did, and it ran perfectly sweetly with the repair that Precious had made.

"I think you should come and sit with us in the front," said Mma Poletsi. "As a reward for what you've done."

Everybody agreed that this was well-deserved, and so Precious made the rest of the journey in comfort, snuggling up against Mma Poletsi in the cab while the sun dropped down below the horizon. She felt proud and happy, and of course excited. Very soon she would be seeing Aunty Bee and finding out what the exciting thing was that her aunt had talked about.

THEY ARRIVED AT EAGLE ISLAND Camp by
night. It was very different from home,
where the lights of houses and of cars
meant that it was never really dark; here
in the bush there was complete darkness,
with only one or two tiny pinpricks of light
showing from a campfire or a hut. Precious
was sleepy, and Aunty Bee said that she
should go straight to bed.

"You'll see where you are when you wake
up in the morning," she said. "There'll be
plenty of time to explore then."

Her aunt had laid out a mattress on the
floor in her own room, and Precious found
this very comfortable. She closed her eyes

23

and in less than a minute she was fast asleep, not waking up until the first rays of the sun came through the window the next day.

She looked about her, half-forgetting where she was. But then she remembered, and got up to dress herself as quickly as she could. There were sounds coming from the kitchen next door, which meant that Aunty Bee was already preparing breakfast.

She greeted her aunt and sat down at the table. Through the open door of the kitchen she could see that Aunty Bee's house was in the middle of a circle of small buildings that housed the people who worked in the safari camp. Not far away, at the end of a path that ran through a clump of very high trees, was the camp itself. This was made up of thatched huts on the edge of a river, all joined to one another by a raised wooden walkway. It looked like a very exciting place to stay.

Aunty Bee served her a bowl of porridge

and a thick slice of bread spread with jam Aunty Bee had made herself. While Precious was eating this, she listened to the story her aunt had to tell.

"There is something very special happening," Aunty Bee began. "We have some filmmakers arriving today. Everybody is very excited."

Precious felt excited too, and asked what sort of film they were making.

"It's about a man who gets lost in the jungle," said Aunty Bee. "I don't know the full story, but they have lots of people coming with cameras and lights and all the other things they need to make a film. We're going to be very busy."

Aunty Bee would have more cooking to do, she said, once all the film people arrived. "You'll have to entertain yourself," she said to Precious. "But please be careful. Don't wander away from the camp by yourself—there are plenty of wild animals around here."

Precious promised that she would be very careful. "I won't go near any elephants," she said. "And I'll keep well away from lions too!"

After they had finished their breakfast, Aunty Bee went off to work, promising to return just before lunchtime to check that everything was all right. There were other children nearby, she said, and she was sure that Precious would meet them.

Precious said goodbye to her aunt and waved to her as she made her way along the path to the main camp. Then she did a bit of cleaning-up to help Aunty Bee, before she went outside to explore. She hoped that she would see some of the other children, but there seemed to be none around. So she decided to go down to the edge of the river, which was not very far away from the staff houses.

That was her first mistake—and it was a bad one. Nobody had warned her about hippos—perhaps they had meant to do so and had forgotten, or perhaps they just

thought that she knew what dangerous and bad-tempered creatures they could be.

Certainly the hippo that Precious came across was not in a good temper. As she came down to the edge of the river, the hippo suddenly rose from the water, fixed her with an angry stare, and opened his great mouth to issue a resounding grunt. It was a very frightening noise:

For a moment Precious stood quite still, too petrified to move. Then, turning on her heels, she ran back up the path as fast as her legs would carry her. Which was quite fast, of course, as most people run rather quickly when they meet an angry hippo. And as she ran round a corner, she bumped straight into a boy about her age who was standing in the path wondering what the noise was all about.

"There's a hippo down there!" shouted Precious, struggling to recover her breath.

The boy, whose name was Khumo (you say it KOO-MO), did not seem surprised.

"Oh, that's just Harry," he said. "He's always down there. He's a very lazy hippo and has never chased anybody."

Precious was relieved, but she had still had a dreadful fright. "He looked very fierce," she said.

Khumo smiled. "Well, let's leave him in peace. Why don't you come with me now and see what's happening in the camp. It's something very exciting. There's a lion."

Precious was not sure that she wanted

to meet a lion so soon after her encounter with the hippo, but Khumo seemed to know what he was doing. So she followed him back along the track, wondering all the while what would await them when they reached the camp.

A S THEY MADE THEIR WAY to the main camp, Khumo told Precious about the lion.

"Most of the lions around here are wild ones," he said. "This one, though, is not from here. He came with the filmmakers. He's an actor lion."

Precious looked puzzled and asked her new friend to explain.

"They brought him with them," he said. "He's tame. They're going to use him in the film they're making."

Precious nodded; now she understood. She had heard about dogs that had been

trained to act in films—to fetch things and
so on—but she had never heard of a lion
doing this.

"Are you sure he's completely tame?"
she asked nervously. They were now
getting close to the camp and she could
see people milling around. She could also
see a large cage in which something—and
it must have been the actor lion—was
moving.

"Everybody says he is," Khumo replied.
"Anyway, we'll soon find out. It looks as if
they're going to let him out of his cage."

They had now reached the camp and
were standing with some of the film people
near the lion's cage. There was a tall man
wearing a large brown hat who seemed to
be in charge of the lion.

"Let him out now, Tom," said somebody
to this man, who then stepped forward and
opened the door of the cage.

Precious gave a shiver as the great lion
came out into the sunlight. Nobody else,
though, seemed to be worried, and Tom,
the man with the large hat, went forward
to pat the lion on the head.

"You see?" said Khumo. "He's tame. You couldn't do that to a lion who wasn't tame, could you?"

Precious had to agree that you could not.

The children watched as the film crew set about their work. Tom took the lion, called Teddy by everyone, to the tree and told him to sit under it.

"Sit, Teddy," he said. And Teddy, like a well-trained dog, sat down obediently. The

scene they were filming had two actors walking across a piece of ground and seeing the lion, sitting under a tree.

There were cameras mounted on trolleys and there was a lot of shouting and rushing about. Nobody seemed to mind Precious and Khumo watching, and at one point somebody even asked them to hold on to a cable while it was being wound up. This made them feel very important—as if they were members of the film crew itself. And later on, when everybody took a break, the two children were handed large mugs of sweet tea and the fattest fat cake they had ever seen. A fat cake is a special treat in Botswana.

It tastes just like a doughnut, but more delicious, if that is possible.

Precious and Khumo ate their fat cakes and were licking the sugar off their fingers when Tom came over to ask them to help.

"We want to film Teddy standing up suddenly and looking at something in the grass," he said. "Would you mind hiding in the grass, and then, when I give you the signal, making some sort of sound to attract his attention. Maybe a sort of clucking sound, as if you're a guinea fowl.

Lions like guinea fowl, you know, and that sound will be bound to interest him."

They felt very important to have a job to do, and they both went off to hide in the grass as Tom had asked them. As they lay there, Precious suddenly had a worrying thought.

"What if he thinks we really are guinea fowl?" she whispered to Khumo.

"He won't," said Khumo. "He's a very clever lion."

"I hope so," said Precious. "Because if he really thought we were guinea fowl, then he might pounce on us."

They waited quietly, the only sound being that of their beating hearts. Precious thought that her heart was beating rather loudly—and so did Khumo. That's the trouble about being frightened—you may be as quiet as you can manage, but your heart doesn't seem to take much notice.

"Right," called Tom. "Please attract Teddy's attention now."

Precious and Khumo both started to make the noise that a guinea fowl makes. It sounded a bit like the noise a hen makes, only it was a bit more . . . well, spotted.

At first Teddy did nothing.

"Perhaps he's feeling a bit sleepy," whispered Khumo. "I think we should be a bit louder."

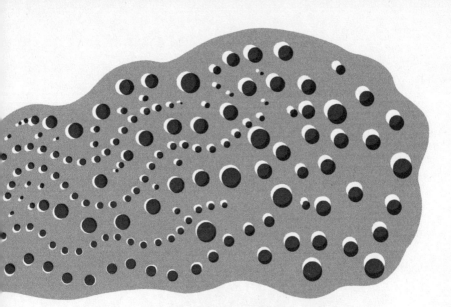

They raised the volume of the noise and, sure enough, Teddy's ears started to prick up. Then he sat up and looked with interest in their direction. After that, things happened very quickly—so quickly, in fact, that neither Precious nor Khumo had much time to react.

With one great bound, Teddy reached the edge of the clump of tall grass in which the two children were hiding. Then, with another not quite so long bound, he was upon them.

Precious closed her eyes. If you were

going to be eaten by a lion, then she
thought it was probably best not to see
what was happening. But then she felt
a rather rough, wet tongue licking at
her face, moving on to her neck, finally
getting to her knees. It was a bit like being
tickled, and she could not stop herself from
laughing.

Teddy had pounced on them not to eat them or to scratch them, but to play. Now he was lying on the ground, his feet up in the air, inviting them to scratch his stomach. It was very funny.

Tom was very pleased with what his cameras had seen, and they all went back to the camp for tea and more fat cakes.

"You did very well," Tom said to Precious and Khumo. "Please stay with us and help us for the rest of the day."

"Certainly," said Precious.

And Khumo, without any hesitation, said the same thing.

CHAPTER FIVE

IT PROVED TO BE AN EXCITING DAY. And the day after that was exciting too, as there was filming to be done deep in the forest. That meant a long ride in a truck—with Teddy—along a very bumpy and overgrown track.

Tom was very pleased with the work that Precious and Khumo did, and he made sure that at the end of the day they were rewarded with an envelope full of money. That suited them very well, as they were both saving for things, and the money would be very helpful for that.

But then, at the end of the second day, just after they had returned to the camp

and Precious was back in Aunty Bee's
house, they heard the sound of people
shouting and calling. Something had
clearly happened, and when Precious and
her aunt went outside, they found out
what it was.

"Teddy's disappeared!" shouted one of
the film men. "We don't know where he is."

Precious joined the group of people
from the camp who started looking for
the missing lion. They searched under
the trucks and vans; they searched in the
sheds where they kept supplies; they even
looked under the beds in some of the camp
huts just in case he had decided to find a

hiding place there. But there was no sign of him—Teddy, it seemed, had vanished into thin air.

Darkness came down like a curtain. Now it was too late to search anymore, and they all had to go to bed hoping that in the morning he would come out from wherever he was hiding in time for that day's filming.

"He'll turn up," said Aunty Bee. "Or at least I hope he'll turn up."

The next morning, when the sun rose up over the tops of the trees like a great red ball, Precious went outside to look for Teddy. She studied the ground, as her father had taught her to do, for any sign that a lion had walked that way, but there was nothing. She saw the footprints of a small family of warthogs,

but nothing that looked like the large tracks that a lion leaves behind.

After breakfast, when she went down to the camp with Khumo, they saw Tom sitting unhappily beneath a tree, his head sunk in his hands.

"I don't know what to do," he said. "Without Teddy, we'll have to change the whole story of our film."

Precious felt very sorry for the director. It was not easy to make a film, and when one of the stars decides to disappear it must make it even more difficult.

"I think we should try to help him," she said to Khumo. "I think we should go and look for him."

Khumo was uncertain. "But will they let us?" he asked.

"I can ask Aunty Bee," said Precious.

She went to her aunt and explained what she and Khumo wanted to do. "If we are very, very, very careful," she said, "will you let us go off and look for the missing lion?"

Aunty Bee looked doubtful. "There are rather a lot of elephants about," she said. "And hippos too. Not to mention all those snakes . . ."

"We won't go near any of them," said Precious. "I promise."

Aunty Bee had a canoe. She did not use it very much, but it still floated and as far as she knew there were no holes in it, which was a good thing, as holes in any sort of boat are not a very good idea.

"I suppose you can take my canoe," she said after a while. "But keep well away from hippos."

"We will," said Precious, as she ran off to tell Khumo the good news.

They set off about an hour later. Precious had packed some sandwiches—enough for both of them—and she also brought a spare hat, and a compass to use in case they got lost. Khumo brought a bag of toffees, a small box of bandages, a box of

matches, and two bottles of water. They
had everything they needed.

The canoe was an old-fashioned one,
made of wood and propelled through the
water with two stout paddles. It was a
little bit wobbly, but canoes often are and
you quickly get used to them. Soon they
were slipping through the water of the
great river, and after half an hour they
were well into the wild forests and plains
that surrounded the camp.

They looked about them very carefully as they made their way. There was plenty to see on the banks of the river. There were great trees from which vines hung down like swinging ropes. There were slippery patches of mud used by crocodiles to launch

themselves into the water. There were places where herds of zebra and antelopes came nervously down to the edge of the river to drink, watching all the time for lions that might creep up behind them, or crocodiles that might lurk in the water in

front of them. It was dangerous being a zebra or antelope as there were plenty of other creatures around about who might imagine that you were just right for their breakfast, lunch, or even their dinner.

After a few hours of paddling, they stopped on a small island in the middle of the river. Beaching the canoe, they found some comfortable grass on which to have their picnic of the sandwiches that Precious

had prepared. They were very hungry, as paddling a canoe takes a lot of energy and breakfast had been some time ago.

They had just finished their last sandwich when Precious noticed a movement on the riverbank opposite their island.

"What was that?" she asked Khumo, shading her eyes from the bright glare of the sun. "I think I saw something over there."

Khumo rose to his feet—slowly, so

as not to disturb whatever it was that
Precious had seen. "I can't see anything,"
he said. But then, quite suddenly, he did
see something, and it made him take in his
breath with a gasp.

"Lions," he whispered. "A whole pride of
them."

"Sit down," whispered Precious. "We
don't want them to see us."

They remained quite still as the pride
of lions made its way down to the water to
drink. There were six of them altogether,

and it did not take long for Precious and Khumo to identify which one was Teddy.

"That's him," whispered Khumo, pointing to a lion standing at the edge of the group.

Precious saw that it was Teddy. He seemed to be quite happy with his new friends, and they watched them all until the biggest lion, who was also the leader, roared, then they turned round and made their way back into the bush.

Once the lions had gone, Precious and

Khumo pushed their canoe back into the water, climbed into it, and paddled back down the river. They did not take a break on the way back, as they wanted to get to Tom as soon as possible to give him the good news that they had found his missing lion.

CHAPTER SIX

TOM WAS VERY PLEASED.

"Do you remember exactly where you saw the lions?" he asked. "Will you be able to take us to them?"

Khumo looked a bit doubtful. "I think so," he began. "It was where the river went a bit like this . . ." He made a movement of his hands. "And then it went a bit like this . . ." He made another movement to show a change of direction.

Tom looked worried. Rivers were always going like this, and then this, and he was not sure whether Khumo's directions would be good enough. But he did not know, of course, that Precious was the girl who was destined to become Botswana's most famous detective, and that she had stored away in her memory every detail of the trip down the river.

"Excuse me," she said. "I know exactly where the spot is. It is after the river turns to the left just before you reach a very old tree that has half-fallen into the water. There are some sand banks in the middle of the river that are about as deep as the top of my knees, and then there is an island that has a bush at one end, a clump of rocks at the other, and an anthill in the middle. The lions came down to drink on the shore right on the other side. So they'll be somewhere near there."

Tom looked impressed. "You are a very
observant girl," he said. "I'm sure that will
help us to find the place."

Precious smiled modestly. She was not
at all boastful, and she wanted to make
sure that Khumo would get some of the
praise that was being given. "Khumo
helped a lot," she said.

Tom thanked Khumo too, and it was agreed that once everybody was ready, they would set off once again to see if they could find Teddy. Precious was not sure how they would manage to get him back— particularly if he was having a good time with his new lion friends—but Tom seemed to think this would not be too hard.

"He's a very tame lion," he said. "I'm sure that once he finds that he has to hunt for his food and not have it delivered to him in a big dish, he will be less eager to stay out in the wild."

There was enough time before they left for Precious to go and tell her aunt all about their adventure. Aunty Bee was relieved that they had got home without getting into any trouble, and was very proud of the fact that they had managed to find Teddy. She was perfectly happy for Precious to go out again, this time with Tom and the other people from the film crew.

"They'll look after you," she said. And

then she stopped and thought. "Or maybe *you* will be the one to look after *them*."

Precious smiled. "We'll see," she said.

Aunty Bee looked at her fondly. "You know something?" she said. "Your father said that he thought you had the makings of a great detective. And I think he might be right."

They took a much bigger boat this time—large enough for ten people to sit in quite comfortably and not get at all wet. This boat had an engine, and it made a throaty roar as they set off from the camp. Precious looked back and waved to her aunt, and Khumo waved too, continuing to do so until they rounded a bend in the river and lost sight of the camp.

It did not take them long to make the trip. There were quite a few islands, but Tom was able to identify the right one from the description that Precious had given. Now they were in sight of the place on the shore where the lions had been, and were able to steer their boat gently in to the muddy bank.

They got their feet a bit wet as they went ashore, but the water was warm and that did not matter.

"We must be very quiet now," said Tom, putting a finger to his lips. "Lions have very good hearing and we don't want them to take fright and run away."

Once everybody was on dry land and the boat had been firmly tied to a tree trunk at the edge of the water, the whole party began to walk very slowly and carefully through the thick grass and scrub bush. Tom led the way, and then came one of

his men, and behind them were Precious and Khumo. The other men who had come with them brought up the rear, looking anxiously around them from time to time.

"You have to be very careful when looking for lions," Tom whispered. "Sometimes when you are looking for a lion, the lion creeps round behind you and then, before you know what's happened, you're being stalked by the lion rather than the other way round."

Precious gave a shiver when she heard this. She did not like the thought of a lion creeping up behind her.

"Don't worry," said Khumo. "Tom will be very careful."

"I hope so," said Precious.

They walked for about an hour. "No sign of anything yet," said Tom. "Have you seen any tracks?"

Precious shook her head. "Only old ones," she said. "I think lions must have been here once, but I think it was quite a few days ago—maybe even weeks."

She had just finished saying this when she noticed something. It was not something that most people would notice, but you have to remember that she was a detective-in-training and so she saw things that other people walked right past.

"Wait," she said, her voice low. "Look at this."

The whole line of people came to a stop.

"What have you found?" asked Tom.

Precious pointed to a bush at the side of the rough track they were following. One of the branches had been bent back so that it had snapped. There was still fresh sap where the break had happened.

"Something passed by this way not all that long ago," she said. "Some big animal."

"But it could have been anything," said Tom. "A zebra. A buffalo. Anything."

Precious was now down on her hands and knees, examining the ground. "No," she said. "It was a lion. Several lions, in fact. Look at these."

Tom and Khumo, along with the other men who were with them, now bent down to look at the ground where Precious was pointing.

Khumo, whose father was a game scout

who had taught him how to track wild animals, saw what his friend meant. "Precious is right," he said. "Lions went this way—and only a few minutes ago."

At the news that the lions had been there only a few minutes earlier, Tom and his men looked a bit anxious.

"I hope they're not too close," said one of the men, giving a little shiver as he spoke.

"We'll soon find out," said Precious. "Let's follow their tracks—keeping a careful lookout, of course."

"A *very* careful lookout," said Tom.

THEY WENT FORWARD SLOWLY, looking down at the ground very carefully before they put down their feet. This was so that they should not step on a twig that might snap and give them away to any creature that was listening. And lions do listen for anything that is coming their way. They are also very watchful animals, even if they are big and fierce and have large teeth that are very good at biting. . . . Precious did not like to think of that, and neither, I imagine, do you.

It was Precious who spotted them first. At first she thought it was just one of those tricks that your eyes can play. She thought it might just be a branch swaying in the breeze, or the shadow of a tiny cloud moving across the ground. But then she realized that it was neither of these, and that what she was looking at was a lion.

Once she knew that, then in an instant she saw all the rest. She saw that what looked like a pile of brown leaves on the ground was actually a young lion lying with his head on his front paws. And then what looked like a bendy branch in front of a bush was in fact a large lioness that was

standing quite still looking up at the sky.
Altogether she saw six lions, and they
were not far away, really probably not
much farther than you or I could throw a
small stone.

She reached out to tap Khumo on the
shoulder. He turned round, looked where
she was pointing, and then he let out a
very low whistle to alert Tom.

"Over there," whispered Khumo.
"Look!"

Precious and Khumo both knew that

they were safe as long as they made no sudden movements or sounds. This was because the wind was blowing from the direction of the lions. Had it been blowing the other way, then the lions would have smelled them very easily. Lions have a good sense of smell, and can tell when people or other animals are nearby just by lifting their great lion noses into the air and sniffing at the breeze.

Tom studied the lions and the way they were lying around resting. After a few moments, he whispered to Precious and Khumo, telling them what his plan was.

"Teddy is right on the edge of the pride," he said. "See him over there?"

They looked. Sure enough, Teddy was some distance away from the others, under the shade provided by a tree. He seemed to be having his afternoon nap.

"I'm going to creep up toward him," Tom went on. "There's quite a bit of cover, and that means that they won't see me.

Once I reach him, he'll remember me, of course, and will come back here with me. He always obeys me, especially if I offer him one of his lion treats."

He showed them a large biscuit—rather like a dog biscuit—that he was holding in his right hand.

"Isn't that a bit dangerous?" asked Precious. "What if the other lions see you? What then?"

"They won't see me," said Tom. "I will be very careful."

Precious glanced at Khumo, who shrugged. If this was what Tom wanted to do, then they could not do anything to stop him. After all, Tom was an adult, and it is often rather difficult for children to stop adults from doing things once they have made up their minds to do it.

Dropping to his hands and knees, Tom began to crawl through the undergrowth. He moved very slowly, and he was well-covered by the grass and bushes, so Precious stopped worrying quite so much that he would be seen. Perhaps Tom really knew what he was doing after all, she thought.

But then something dreadful happened. It was so dreadful that Precious almost gave a shriek when she discovered it. Fortunately she did not, because that would have made matters a whole lot worse.

What happened was that she suddenly saw that at the other edge of the clearing another lion had woken up and was

showing his face. That face was Teddy's—
she was absolutely sure of it. The lion that
Tommy was now approaching looked like
Teddy, but that was all. He was definitely
not the tame actor lion, but was a wild lion
that would not be very interested in being
offered a lion treat by a man on his hands
and knees. For such a lion, it would not
be the biscuit, but the man himself who
would seem like a tasty afternoon snack.

Precious had to act quickly. She
could not call out to Tom, as that would
disturb all the other lions, making them
immediately come bounding toward them.
So she would have to do something quite
different—which is what she now did.

First she picked up a stone. Then, half-rising, she made her best imitation of a guinea fowl.

Then, with every ounce of strength she had, she threw the stone up into the air to the other side of the clearing—well away from where Tom was crawling through the grass.

At the sound of the guinea fowl, all the lions in the pride rose to their feet and looked about them with interest. Then, when the stone landed in a thick clump of bush well away from the humans, the lions all bounded off to investigate. Lions, as you know, cannot resist guinea fowl and the thought that there might be a plump guinea fowl so close to them was just too much of a temptation.

Tom saw what was happening. The

moment the lion toward which he was crawling rose to his feet, he knew that he had made a terrible mistake. He froze, not moving while the great lion rushed past him. Then, when the danger was over and the lions were all sniffing about in the bush for a guinea fowl that was not there, Tom crawled back to join the others as fast as his knees would carry him.

"Thank you," he whispered to Precious as they made their way hurriedly back down the track toward the boat. "You saved my life, you know."

He thanked her again when they reached the boat, and he repeated his thanks when they arrived back at the camp. That was exactly what he should have done. If somebody saves your life, then you should thank him or her at least three times. And if you are particularly grateful, you can say thank you a fourth time, which is what he did that night over dinner round the camp fire. Precious had been invited and sat there modestly while Tom told the story. Then everybody clapped and cheered, which made Precious feel a bit embarrassed. She was a modest girl, you see, and she had simply done what she had to do.

THE NEXT DAY there was a meeting of Tom and all the film crew. Precious and Aunty Bee were invited, as was Khumo.

"We are going to have to try to get Teddy back again," said Tom. "This time we are going to take a famous lion catcher with us. He will be arriving with his net just before lunchtime."

Precious looked at the ground. She did not like the thought of Teddy being caught in a net. That would have been a very frightening experience for any lion, particularly for a gentle lion like Teddy.

Tom noticed that Precious looked upset.

"Is there anything wrong with my plan?" he asked.

Precious bit her lip. She was not sure how to say what she wanted to say, but then Aunty Bee said something that helped make up her mind. "It's always better to speak the things that are in your heart," she whispered. "Never be too shy to do that."

Precious knew that her aunt was right. And her father had told her the same thing too. "Don't bite your tongue and say nothing when you feel that you have to speak. People respect a person who says what she thinks."

Now she looked up. "I don't think you should catch him," she said. "I think that he's happy being free."

This was greeted with silence.

"But he's an actor," said Tom at last. "His place is with us—in the films. He has a job to do!"

"His place is with other lions," said Precious. "That is where he will be happiest. Lions like to be with other lions—that is well known."

Tom opened his mouth to say something else, but then he closed it.

"I think we should leave him," Precious went on. "Those other lions will teach him how to hunt and to live in the wild again. He will learn how to sleep under the stars. He will learn how to wash his paws in rivers. He will learn how to roll about in a dust bath and jump up in the air to catch a guinea fowl as it flies from the grass. He will learn a lot of things that lions need to

know." She paused. "That *real* lions need to know."

She stopped, because everybody was looking at her.

"Is that all?" Tom finally asked.

"Yes," she said. "I hope you don't think me rude, but that is what I really feel."

Tom waited a moment before replying.

"I think you're right," he said. "You've made me see it from Teddy's point of view—from the lion's point of view. I've never done that before—I've always thought of myself. Now I know I'm wrong."

"I agree," said Tom's assistant.

"And I agree too," said the head cameraman. "We've already got plenty of shots of lions that we can use."

Precious thought of something else. "But there's one other thing," she said. "I think we should go back there to say goodbye. We can do that from the boat—it won't be dangerous if we do it that way."

They all agreed, and so a few hours later they set off again, this time taking Aunty Bee with them. She had time to make some especially delicious sandwiches that they ate as the boat drifted down the river toward the place where the lions liked to drink from the edge of the water.

The lions were there. This time it was Khumo who saw them first, and he excitedly pointed them out to everybody else on the boat. Teddy was with them—there was no mistaking him— and when they approached in their boat, keeping a safe distance away, he came

down to the edge of the water and sniffed at the air.

For a few moments Precious wondered whether he was going to try to swim out to see them. He looked at them, and he moved his head up and down a bit as if he were greeting them. Then he let out a little roar. It was not an unfriendly roar; it was more of a *hello, how are you?* roar rather than a *stay away from me!* roar.

Tom raised a hand to wave to Teddy. The lion and the man looked at each other for

quite a few minutes, as if they were both remembering all the time they had spent together. Then, rather sadly, in the way in which you would leave a good friend, Teddy turned round and began to walk back to the new life he had found for himself.

That was the last night that Precious was to spend with her aunt. The following day, she was to go back home with the people who had brought her up in their truck. She was sad to be leaving Aunty Bee, but she had plenty of friends back home to whom she was looking forward to telling the story of her adventures. Khumo was sorry to see her go, but he promised to write to her and said that he hoped one day he would see her again. He knew that she was already a detective and that she would become an even better detective as the years went by.

"Perhaps you'll teach me how to be your assistant," he said. "Only if you've got the time, of course."

"Perhaps," said Precious.

That night, asleep on the floor of her aunt's room, with the sounds of the African night coming in through the window, she dreamed that she was out in the bush. In this dream she was walking along a path when she suddenly came upon a lion, and this was a lion called Teddy. And he smiled at her, in a curious, lion-like way before he ambled off back into the grass. It was not long grass, and she could see him quite

well in the dream as he bounded off into the distance.

"Goodbye!" she whispered under her breath.

And he half-turned his head, and looked back at her, and said something that she did not quite catch. She did not know what it was, but she did know that it was something happy.

GEOGRAPHY AND PEOPLE OF BOTSWANA

BOTSWANA is located toward the bottom of Africa and is roughly the size of Texas. It is a wide dry land with lots of amazing things to see. The capital is Gaborone. Pronounced Ha-bo-ro-nee.

SETSWANA is the language spoken in most of Botswana. Most people also speak English, and newspapers, for example, will be in both languages.

THE KALAHARI is a semi-desert, which occupies the central and western parts of Botswana. It is a great stretch of dry grass and thorn trees where very few people live.

THE BUSH—the rural, undeveloped land of Botswana, which is far from civilization.

OKAVANGO—the great river in the north that flows the wrong way—instead of flowing from land to sea, the water goes from the ocean to the heart of Africa where it is absorbed into the sands of the Kalahari.

WILDLIFE—Botswana has a wide variety of wild animals, including lions, elephants, zebras, buffalo, leopards, hippos, hyenas, baboons, snakes, monkeys, and many more.

MMA is the term used to address a woman, and may be placed before her name. It is pronounced "ma" (with a long a). This is what Precious and her classmates call their teacher.

READER'S GUIDE
The Mystery of the Missing Lion
by Alexander McCall Smith

ABOUT THE BOOK:

Precious Ramotswe goes to visit her aunt who works at a safari camp in northern Botswana. The journey takes a full day and Precious must be accompanied by an adult. A film crew has come to the camp to make a movie, bringing with them a tame lion to use in the film. When the lion disappears, Precious and her new friend Khumo take a canoe into the delta to see if they can find the missing lion. But will the lion return easily to his tamer, or has he found a new family?

BOOK TALK:

Precious Ramotswe loves an adventure, almost as much as she loves to solve a mystery. She finds both on her visit to her Aunty Bee who works at a safari camp that is a long day's journey from where she lives. The camp is in the Okavango Delta, a place teeming with wild animals—angry hippos, huge elephants, dangerous crocodiles, and prides of lions. Precious and her new friend Khumo are helping a film crew make a movie with the tame lion the crew has brought to the camp. When the lion disappears, Precious and Khumo set out to find him. With Khumo's help Precious uses her detection skills to figure out where he can be. But will Precious dare to tell the adults what she feels is the right thing to do once they know where he is?

PRE-READING ACTIVITY:

Locate the country of Botswana on a map of Africa. Locate the Okavango Delta on a map of Botswana. Learn about the geography and wildlife of Botswana, and especially the lions. What did you learn from your research that you found especially interesting?

DISCUSSION QUESTIONS:

1. Why is Aunty Bee different from other aunts? What is special about the presents Aunty Bee has sent to Precious? Why is Precious so excited about visiting her at this time?

2. What is a safari camp? What would you do if you went to a safari camp? What would you expect to learn there?

3. How does Precious travel to the camp? How does she help Mr. Poletsi when the truck breaks down? What does this tell you about Precious and how she solves problems?

4. What is Aunty Bee's surprise when Precious arrives at the safari camp? How does Precious meet Khumo?

5. Why is Precious worried about the job that Tom gives them to help with the filming? What makes Khumo feel calm about their job? Which one of them is right about how the lion Teddy will behave?

6. How did Teddy's disappearance affect the making of the film?

7. Why does Aunty Bee let Precious and Khumo take her canoe? Which animals do they need to fear the most as they set off to hunt for Teddy?

8. How do Precious's detective skills help them to find Teddy? What skill does Khumo use to help the search?

9. How did Precious and Khumo know they were safe when they first spotted the lions?

10. What does Precious do that saves Tom's life? How does Tom show his gratitude?

11. Why does Precious think Teddy should be left in the wild? Discuss Aunty Bee's comment: "It's always better to speak the things that are in your heart." (p. 82)

12. Why does Tom accept what Precious tells him? How do they know they made the right decision to let Teddy go back to the wild?

CURRICULUM CONNECTIONS:

1. Geography:
The story takes place in a particular part of Botswana—the Okavango Delta. Look up the meaning of the word "delta." What can you learn about this area that is unique and special? How is the Okavango Delta different from other parts of Botswana?
http://www.botswanatourism.co.bw/welcome-botswana

2. Science/Biology–The Animal Kingdom:
Look up information about the indigenous animals in the Okavango Delta region of Botswana. Discuss how the animals in this area live and interact with the environment.
http://www.okavangodeltasafaris.com/wildlife.html

Look up information about the lions of Botswana. What can you learn about this animal that is not included in the story? Compare what you learn from researching the lions in factual sources to what you can learn about them from the story.
http://okavango-delta.botswana.co.za/lions-okavango.html

3. Language Arts:
Write a description of your favorite character in the book. What questions would you like to ask this character about his or her life in Botswana?

Rewrite the story from the point of view of Teddy, the lion, or write another chapter for the story about Teddy adapting to his new life in the wilderness.

4. Social Studies:
   In an interview with his publisher, the author, Alexander McCall Smith, says this:

   "I very much hope that American readers will get a glimpse of the remarkable qualities of Botswana. It is a very special country and I think that it particularly chimes with many of the values which Americans feel very strongly about—respect for the rule of law and for individual freedom. I hope that readers will also see in these portrayals of Botswana some of the great traditional virtues in Africa— in particular, courtesy and a striking natural dignity."

   What have you learned about the country of Botswana and its people from reading this book? How is the countryside in Botswana different from where you live? Describe the safari camp and the job that Aunty Bee has at the camp. What other jobs would there be for people who work at the camp?

Discussion Guide prepared by Connie Rockman, Youth Literature Consultant and adjunct professor of children's and young adult literature.

PRECIOUS RAMOTSWE
MYSTERIES FOR YOUNG READERS

THE GREAT CAKE MYSTERY

When a piece of cake goes missing from Precious Ramotswe's classroom, a traditionally built young boy is tagged as the culprit. Precious, however, is not convinced. She sets out to find the real thief. Along the way she learns that your first guess isn't always right. She also learns how to be a detective.

THE MYSTERY OF MEERKAT HILL

Precious has a new mystery to solve! When her friend's family's most valuable cow vanishes, Precious must devise a plan to find the missing animal. But she needs the help of the family's pet meerkat to solve the case. Will she succeed and what obstacles will she face on her path?

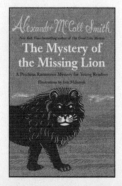

THE MYSTERY OF THE MISSING LION

Precious gets a very special treat: A trip to visit her Aunty Bee at a safari camp. On her first day there, a new lion arrives. But this is no average lion: Teddy is an actor-lion who came with a film crew. When Teddy escapes, Precious and her resourceful new friend Khumo decide to use their detective skills and help track down the lion and find out where he has gone.

Illustration © Iain McIntosh

THE NO. 1 LADIES' DETECTIVE AGENCY SERIES

**Precious Ramotswe mysteries
for adults. Read them all.
"There is no end to the pleasure."**
—*The New York Times Book Review*

**The No. 1 Ladies' Detective
Agency**—Volume 1

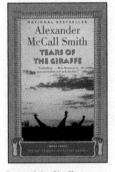

Tears of the Giraffe
—Volume 2

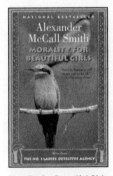

Morality for Beautiful Girls
—Volume 3

**The Kalahari Typing School
for Men**—Volume 4

The Full Cupboard of Life
—Volume 5

**In the Company of Cheerful
Ladies**—Volume 6

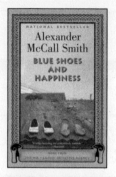

Blue Shoes and Happiness
—Volume 7

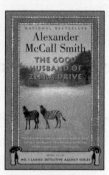

**The Good Husband
of Zebra Drive**—Volume 8

**The Miracle at Speedy
Motors**—Volume 9

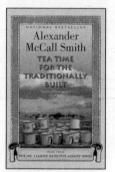

**Tea Time for the
Traditionally Built**—Volume 10

**The Double Comfort
Safari Club**—Volume 11

**The Saturday Big Tent
Wedding Party**—Volume 12

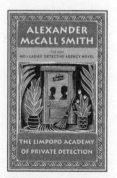

**The Limpopo Academy of
Private Detection**—Volume 13

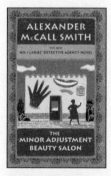

**The Minor Adjustment
Beauty Salon**—Volume 14

**The Handsome Man's
De Luxe Café**—Volume 15